I WANT A BROTHER OR SISTER

by Astrid Lindgren

pictures by Ilon Wikland

translated by Barbara Lucas

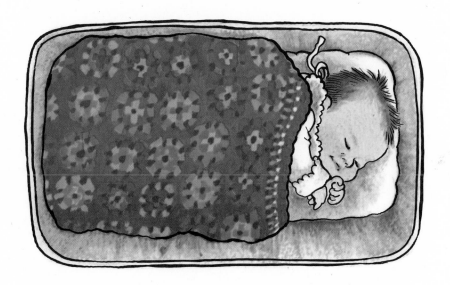

ISBN 0-15-239387-0

HARCOURT BRACE JOVANOVICH   NEW YORK AND LONDON   HBJ

Now Peter is this big.

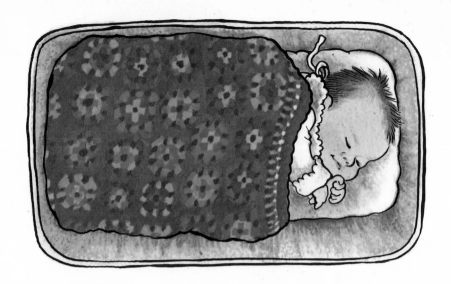

But once he was this little.

Then he could not walk or talk. But he could cry! When he cried, his mama would come and pick him up from his bed and put her cheek against his and tell him that he was the sweetest baby in the world. And when Peter was hungry, he would get milk from his mother. Every night she would bathe him in his small tub. Then Peter would splash like a little fish, and sometimes he would try to eat the soap. Papa thought it was fun to watch Peter take a bath, for Peter was surely the sweetest baby in the world! And Mama and Papa loved him very, very much.

Later Peter grew bigger and could walk and talk and eat meatballs and build with his blocks and play with the children on his street.

At the playground he sometimes met a boy called Jan. One day Jan came pushing a baby carriage, looking quite pleased. In the carriage was a little baby, and Jan said, "This is my brother."

"Oh," said Peter.

"Do you have any brothers or sisters?" asked Jan.

"No, but I have a truck at home that I can put my blocks in," said Peter.

"It's better to have a brother or sister," said Jan. "Then you get to push the baby carriage."

"Pooh," said Peter.

But as soon as he got home, he said to his mama,
"I want a brother or sister."

Then his mother said something amazing. "You *will*
get a brother or sister."

Peter was astonished. Usually he had to beg much
longer for something he wanted. Before, it had been
a three-wheeler he had begged for. But then Mama
just said, "We'll see. Another time perhaps."

One beautiful day Mama came home from the hospital with Peter's sister. She was a little wrinkled thing that cried. But Peter was happy anyway. He thought it was fun to look at her tiny little fingers and toes. And when she cried "Wa-a-a-h," Peter imitated her and cried "Wa-a-a-h" also.

"Her name is Lena," said Mama.

Lena could not walk or talk, only cry. When she cried, Mama came and picked her up from her bed and put her cheek against hers and told her that she was the sweetest baby in the world. And Peter listened to every word. When Lena was hungry, she would get milk from her mother. Every night she got a bath in her small tub, and Papa loved her very, very much.

But Peter did not like Lena at all when he thought about it. It was not any fun to have a sister. And it was amazing that Mama and Papa could love a baby who only cried. But they did love her—that was quite clear. Maybe they even liked her more than they liked Peter. In fact, he began to believe they did, and when he believed that, he became very angry with Lena.

"How dumb I was to say I wanted to have a sister," he thought, "when I could have had a three-wheeler instead."

Then he thought that perhaps he could trade Lena for a three-wheeler, or else sell her for enough money to buy a three-wheeler. "But who would want her?" he asked himself, and he gave her a slap as she lay on a blanket on the floor.

Mama came and grabbed his arm and said that he should be ashamed to hit his little sister. And then Peter got even madder at Lena, and at Mama, too, and kicked Mama and had to go and stand in the corner.

Lena cried, and Peter thought that it would be great if she could be hung in a basket outside the window so that he wouldn't have to listen to her cry.

Whenever Mama put Lena in her lap and gave her milk, Peter made as much of a racket as he possibly could so that Mama would have to put Lena down and come and see what he was doing.

One time he took the scissors and cut off almost all his hair. And one time he took a bowl and threw it on the floor with a great crash. Then Mama would come rushing, and that was good, for, after all, she was Peter's mama first, and not Lena's.

One day Peter felt especially sad. He sat on a pillow and cried, for he had decided that Mama and Papa loved only Lena and didn't like him at all. Then Mama came and took him on her knee. It was so soft and warm on Mama's knee, and he liked sitting there very much. Mama cradled him in her arms just as she did with Lena. And she said, "I love you so very, very much, Peter. First I loved my *little* Peter and now I love my *big* Peter."

Then Peter snuggled deeper in Mama's arms and said, "Lena is so dumb!"

"Lena isn't dumb," said Mama. "Lena is little. And little children are very troublesome."

"Yeah . . ." said Peter.

"I thought maybe you could help me tend Lena," said Mama.

Peter's eyes got very big.

"Where shall we send her?" he asked.

"Not send," said Mama, laughing. "Tend—*look after* her. For she is, after all, your sister. We got her for you. You'll have to look after her yourself now."

"Was I troublesome when I was little?" asked Peter after a moment.

"Oh, you were very troublesome," said Mama. "We had to hold you the same way, otherwise you would scream terribly."

Peter thought about this for a while. Then he decided that maybe it was Lena's turn now to be little and troublesome, and that perhaps it was best after all if he did help Mama look after her. And so he did.

He washed Lena's back when she had her bath, held her bath towel for her, tucked her in bed when she was ready to go to sleep, and said, "Now we aren't going to cry, Crybaby!" And Lena would cry and not go to sleep just the same. But it was enough that Peter had asked Lena to be quiet. Mama was so happy that Peter was helping her with Lena.

And when the sun shined, Mama and Peter
went out with Lena, and Peter got to push
the baby carriage. All the children on
the street came and looked and Peter
said, "This is my sister!"

And time passed, and Peter grew this big

and Lena this big.

Then they got a little brother named Mats. He could not walk or talk, only cry. When he cried, Mama came and picked him up from his bed and told him that he was the sweetest baby in the world. Yes, and Peter and Lena listened. When Mats was hungry, he got milk from his mother. Every night he got a bath in his small tub, and Papa and Peter and Lena watched. Mama and Papa and Peter and Lena loved Mats very, very much.

Of course he was little and troublesome, and Mama had to look after him a lot and didn't have much time for Peter and Lena. But that didn't matter. Peter and Lena had pillow fights in the bedroom, and that was fun. And it was a good thing that Peter hadn't traded Lena for a three-wheeler because then he wouldn't have had anyone to play with now.